Slam Dunk
Saturday

*Dedicated to the Haldane Blue Devils,
particularly the 1989 and 1993 boys'
varsity basketball teams*

*With special thanks to Judy Foster,
Eileen Bishop, Joe Carufe, Jesse Merandy,
the students in Mrs. Liberty's 1990–91
second-grade class, the students in
Mrs. Dawson's 1993–94 sixth-grade class,
and my usual sports consultants:
Dan, Dave, and Claudio Marzollo*

—J. M.

Slam Dunk
Saturday

By Jean Marzollo
Illustrated by Blanche Sims

A STEPPING STONE BOOK
Random House New York

Library of Congress Cataloging-in-Publication Data
Marzollo, Jean. Slam dunk Saturday / by Jean Marzollo ; illustrated by Blanche Sims.   p.   cm. "A Stepping stone book." SUMMARY: Billy wants to do well in his school's basketball fund-raiser, but he is intimidated by a loud-mouthed schoolmate.
ISBN 0-679-82366-2 (pbk.) — ISBN 0-679-92366-7 (lib. bdg.)
[1. Basketball—Fiction.   2. Schools—Fiction.   3. Fund raising—Fiction.]
I. Sims, Blanche, ill.   II. Title. PZ7.M3688S1   1994   [Fic]—dc20 91-25988

Manufactured in the United States of America   10 9 8 7 6 5 4 3

Contents

1 A Terrible Playground

Billy Castello caught the ball and looked up at the hoop. Should he shoot? His team really needed points.

Chad Smith jumped in front of him. "No way, Shrimp! No way!" he yelled. Chad was much taller than Billy. His arms were humongous.

Billy threw to Rosie. She aimed, fired, and missed.

Billy and Chad jumped for the rebound. Billy grabbed it, and Chad knocked him down.

"Watch it!" yelled Billy.

"Foul! One and one," said Ace.

Ace was the star of the Spring Town Tigers varsity basketball team. He liked to help out at recess on the elementary school playground. He was the referee for pickup games.

"C'mon, Ace," cried Chad. "That little squirt was in my way!"

"If you foul him, you pay for it," said Ace. "Billy gets a free shot. If he makes it, he gets another one."

Chad held on to the ball.

"Give him the ball," said Ace.

"It was his fault," said Chad. But he threw the ball to Billy.

The foul line on the playground was marked by a crack in the pavement. Billy stepped up to it.

Recess was almost over, and his team was losing. Billy hated losing. He hated being called a squirt. And he hated foul shots. The crooked hoop was a mile away. It was also missing a net.

Billy threw the ball. It didn't even hit the rim.

"Air ball," sang Chad. He caught the rebound and dribbled up the court. "Pass! Pass!" shouted the other kids on his team. But Chad was a ball hog. And ball hogs never pass.

Billy ran up the court as fast as he could. Then— *wham!* He tripped on a tuft of grass and fell. As he went down, Chad went up.

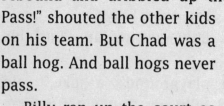

"Did you see that?" Chad shouted. "A perfect jump shot."

It was, but no one cheered.

"Twenty-five to ten. That's it. Game's over," said Ace. "You okay, Billy?"

"Yeah," said Billy, getting up. "But this court is a joke."

"The whole playground's a joke," said Ace. He helped Billy up. "But not for long. With any luck, we'll raise enough money this weekend for a new one."

Basketball Weekend had been organized by the school to raise money for a new playground. The weekend had two main events. Friday night was the big game. Spring Town High School was playing Elmwood High School for the league championship.

The next day was Slam Dunk Saturday, a day of basketball contests. Billy had entered the Shoot-Out Contest. Whoever shot the most baskets in one minute would win.

Chad punched Ace on the shoulder. "You and me, Ace. We'll dominate on Saturday.

Right? Hey, watch out!" Chad knocked the ball away from Ace.

Usually Ace would have reached out and grabbed it back. But this time he didn't. Instead, he started walking toward the school. Billy, Rosie, and their friend Chris walked with him.

Chad chased after the ball. Then he caught up and held it out to Ace. But just as Ace reached over to take the ball, Chad pulled it back.

"Gotcha!" he cried.

Ace didn't laugh.

Chad frowned. Then his face lit up again. "Hey, Ace," he said. "How many baskets do you think you'll make in the high school Shoot-Out Contest?"

Ace shrugged. He seemed to be thinking of something else.

Chad started bragging about how he was the best basketball player. And how he was going to win the Shoot-Out Contest for his age group.

Ace didn't say anything.

"Thinking about Friday night?" Billy asked him.

"You got it," said Ace.

"Gonna be a tough game?" asked Billy.

Ace nodded. "The toughest," he said. "Well, see you later, Champ." Then he headed for the parking lot.

Billy watched him go. He couldn't believe his ears. Ace had called him *Champ!*

As Billy walked into the school, someone pushed him. Who was it? Who else? Billy didn't even have to turn around. He could tell by the voice. It was the ball hog.

"You hear that, guys?" yelled Chad. "Ace called me Champ! That's because I'm going to win on Saturday."

Billy's face got hot. What could he say? *No, stupid, he didn't call* you *Champ. He called* me *Champ!* No one would ever believe him.

Because the fact was, Chad would be the champ.

Today was Monday. Basketball Weekend was coming up fast. The very thought of it now made Billy nervous. Nervous for Ace on Friday. Nervous for himself on Saturday.

2 Free Pizza

After school Billy, Rosie, and Chris walked to Castle Pizza. Billy's father owned the pizza parlor. His last name was Castello, which means "castle" in Italian.

Chris and Rosie climbed up onto stools at the counter. Billy went behind the counter and gave his grandfather a kiss. "Hi, Nonno," he said. "Nonno" is the Italian word for "grandfather."

"*Facciamo due,*" said Nonno. That meant

Nonno wanted two kisses. One on each cheek. Billy kissed his grandfather again.

"Me, too," said his father. Billy went over and kissed his dad Italian-style, too.

It was cool having your father and grandfather own the pizza parlor. Billy could go behind the counter whenever he wanted.

Billy drew three cups of milk from the milk machine. He set them on the counter. Then he carefully put three slices of pizza into the oven. Ever since he had turned nine, he had been allowed to use the oven himself. He had burned himself only once.

Billy, Chris, and Rosie carried their food over to an empty booth. On the wall was a poster for Basketball Weekend. Billy had made it himself. He had painted a huge orange basketball in the middle.

Above the ball he had printed in big letters, "RAISE MONEY FOR THE NEW PLAYGROUND. BUY YOUR TICKETS HERE FOR BASKETBALL WEEKEND!" Underneath, he had added, "Spring Town Game, 8:00 P.M. Friday night! Basketball Contests, 10:00 A.M. Saturday. Enter and have fun!"

Billy now read his poster grimly. "I wish I hadn't entered the Shoot-Out Contest," he said.

"Me, too," said Chris.

"Me, three," said Rosie.

"I'm going to look so stupid," said Billy.

"Me, too," said Chris.

"Me, three," said Rosie.

"Chad has a hoop in his driveway," said Billy. "That's why he's so good."

"He's also huge," added Chris.

"He's also in our age division," said Rosie.

"It's not fair that we have to play against him," grumbled Billy.

"He should be in an older division," said Chris.

"My dad says it doesn't matter who wins," said Billy. "The point is to raise money for the new playground. What matters are your pledges."

"How many pledges do you have?" asked Rosie.

"My mom, my dad, and my grandfather have each pledged a dollar a basket," said Billy. "But if I don't make any baskets, I'll earn zip."

The pizza parlor door opened with a bang. Chad Smith burst in.

"Hey, losers," he said. He slumped into the booth behind theirs. He hung over the back of his seat and watched. Then he opened his mouth and let his tongue hang out.

"Man, oh man, that smells good," he said. "You get it free, Chris? What about you, Rosie?"

Billy, Chris, and Rosie rolled their eyes at each other. But they didn't look up at Chad. They pretended to ignore him.

Chad stretched. "I should get free pizza, too," he said. "After all, I'm going to be the Shoot-Out Champ!"

Chad walked up to the counter. In a really

loud voice he said, "Two slices and a root beer. Compliments of my buddy, Billy Castello!"

Nonno looked across the room at Billy. If Billy shook his head no, Nonno wouldn't give Chad free pizza. Billy didn't know what to do.

"Say no!" whispered Rosie.

"Say no!" whispered Chris.

But Billy wasn't sure. Maybe if he was nice to Chad, Chad wouldn't make fun of him during the Shoot-Out Contest.

So Billy nodded yes. Nonno put two pieces of pizza in the oven. Mr. Castello gave Billy a funny look as he put a cup of root beer on the counter.

"How come you don't coach basketball, Mr. Castello?" asked Chad.

Every year Billy's father coached a baseball team for kids. His team was called Castle Pizza. The year before, thanks to a grand-slam hit by Billy, Castle Pizza had won the town championship. The trophy stood on the cash register.

"You always ask the same question," said Mr. Castello. "And I always give the same answer. Basketball is for tall people. Baseball is for athletes."

"And shrimps," said Chad. Chad was already taller than Mr. Castello.

Mr. Castello laughed. "Athletes," he said. "Some of whom are short. And you're welcome."

"Huh?" said Chad. He looked down at the two pizza slices. "Oh, yeah. I get it. Uh, thanks."

Chad brought his food over to the booth where Billy, Chris, and Rosie were sitting. "Move over, Squirt," he said to Billy.

Billy felt his face get red, but he didn't know what to do, so he moved over. Chad sat down next to Billy. Chad had called him "Squirt" right in his own pizza parlor! Billy was so furious, tears came into his eyes. He opened his eyes wide so the tears would dry up.

He hated the way he cried so easily. He wished he was easygoing, like his father. His father never let rude people get to him. "What am I going to do?" he would say. "Throw everybody who is rude out of the pizza parlor and lose their business?"

But no matter how hard Billy tried to be calm, people like Chad upset him.

Chad hunched over his plate and shoved his pizza into his mouth. "Gimme a napkin," he said as he took another bite.

"Disgusting," said Rosie. But she passed him a napkin.

Chad drank his soda down in one long

gulp. Then he took a deep breath and burped. It was a very long, very loud burp.

"Pitiful," said Rosie.

Chris and Billy tried to ignore Chad.

Chad belched again. Longer and louder.

Billy lifted his slice of pizza. He was just about to take a bite when he heard another burp. The longest and loudest of all. It sounded like a volcano erupting.

Billy was so grossed out that he did a weird thing. He laughed. So did Chris and Rosie. They couldn't help it.

Customers in the pizza parlor were looking over.

"Hey, you kids! Knock it off!" yelled Billy's father from behind the counter. "Billy, it's time to do your homework."

Chad looked at Billy and mimicked his father's voice. "Hey, you kids, knock it off. Billy, it's time to do your homework."

Then Chad got up and strutted out of the pizza parlor. He didn't even clear away his mess.

Billy, Rosie, and Chris didn't feel like laughing any more. Quietly, they threw away their trash. Then they went up to the counter and told Billy's dad they were sorry.

"Don't worry about it," said Mr. Castello. "Just go back and clean up after your friend." The way he said *friend*, they knew he didn't mean it.

The kids looked at Chad's messy stuff. Rosie picked up his cup. It was smeared with tomato sauce. "I'll probably get cooties," she said.

Chris picked up Chad's plate and said, "Yuck."

Billy picked up Chad's greasy napkin with his fingertips and said, "I hate that kid."

3

Nonno's Story

Billy lived with his father and grandfather in an apartment over the pizza parlor. Nonno used to live there alone. But when Billy's parents divorced, Billy and his dad moved in, too. There wasn't much room—just a kitchen, a living room, and two bedrooms.

At first, Billy and his dad had shared a bedroom. But Billy's dad snored too much. After a few weeks, Billy had asked if he could sleep in the kitchen.

It was a weird idea, but it made sense. Billy, his father, and his grandfather ate all their meals down in the pizza parlor. No one ever used the kitchen upstairs. So Billy's dad unplugged the stove and took out the refrigerator. Billy moved in. Since then, he had come to like his funny kitchen bedroom.

Billy now opened the oven. Most of his clothes were stored in the cabinets. The oven was where he kept his baseball books and magazines. Billy was like his dad. Baseball was his number one sport.

All year long Mr. Castello and Billy talked baseball, baseball, baseball. Billy wanted to be a high school baseball star. He wanted to get a baseball scholarship to a good college. And then he wanted to become a pro baseball player. He didn't care if it was for the Mets, the Yankees, the Phillies, the Red Sox, or the White Sox. Just as long as it was a major league team.

Billy sighed. "Forget about baseball," he

told himself. "You need to get as many baskets as you can in the Shoot-Out Contest on
Saturday."

Billy had one basketball book. He took it

out and began to read it carefully. Keep your eye on the hoop, it said. Use your legs. Stay relaxed. Relaxed? No way. Not with Chad the Hog snorting at you behind your back.

Billy lay back on his bed and shut his eyes. What he needed was practice in a private place where Chad couldn't see him.

If he found the right place, he could practice all week. If he practiced all week, he would make at least a few baskets next Saturday. Five or six would be enough. If he made six baskets in one minute, he would make eighteen dollars for the playground. That would be okay. He didn't care about winning. He just didn't want to make a fool of himself.

But six baskets? Billy could hit a grand slam on the baseball field. But could he make six baskets in a minute on the basketball court?

Maybe. But where would he ever find a private place to practice?

With a sigh, Billy turned a page of his basketball book. Before him was a picture of the first two basketball hoops ever made. A man named James Naismith had invented basketball in 1891 in Springfield, Massachusetts. He had used a soccer ball and two peach baskets.

The picture gave Billy an idea. He did his homework quickly and went downstairs. "Nonno," he said. "Are you going to the vegetable market tomorrow morning?"

"*Sì,*" said Nonno. "Yes."

"Can you get me a peach basket?"

"In March?" asked Nonno. "Why you wanna peach basket in March?" Nonno was from Italy. He had lived in America for a long time. But he still spoke with an Italian accent.

"To make a basketball hoop out back. So I can practice for the Shoot-Out Contest. So I won't look stupid in front of Chad."

"You mean that big messy kid?"

"Yeah," said Billy.

Nonno thought for a minute. "I find you basket."

Tuesday afternoon Billy and Nonno went out behind the pizza parlor. Nonno took a peach basket out of his car. He punched the bottom out of it.

Billy and Nonno looked up at an old light pole behind the pizza parlor. "How we gonna get it up there?" asked Nonno.

"I'll get the stepladder," said Billy. "Then I'll climb up."

"No," said Nonno. "Too much trouble. Here, I lift you."

Just then a car pulled up to the curb near the back of the pizza parlor. Ace was at the wheel. He and some other high school basketball players got out. They saw Nonno trying to lift Billy.

"Hold on!" said Ace. "Need some help?"

"Do we ever!" said Billy.

Billy explained what he wanted to do with the basket. Ace and his friends thought the idea was great. So Ace held another player named Ben on his shoulders. Carefully, Ben tied the basket to the pole.

"How do you know how high to tie it?" asked Billy.

"Believe me," said Ace. "We know. You have a basketball, Billy?"

"My friends Rosie and Chris are bringing one later," said Billy. "We're going to practice every day from now until Saturday."

"The sooner you start, the better," said Ace. He got a ball out of his trunk and tossed it to Billy.

"Want a little advice for the Shoot-Out?" asked Ace.

"Sure," said Billy.

"Don't dribble," said Ace. "Take the ball, and go up to the basket. Between now and Saturday, figure out where your best close shot is. Then stand in that place and practice your shot over and over. Let the ball bounce back to you. Don't move unless you have to. Watch."

Ace took the ball and stood about five feet away from the peach basket. He shot the ball and made the basket. The ball bounced back to him. He caught it on a bounce and shot again. He made the basket. He did this a few more times.

Billy was impressed. "That's so cool," he said.

Ace laughed. "I don't know about that. All I know is I'm starved."

"Bravo," said Nonno. "You eat now."

"Sounds good to me," said Ace.

Ace tossed the ball back into his car. Then he and his buddies followed Nonno and Billy into the pizza parlor. They sat at the counter.

"How are you doing?" asked Mr. Castello. He was pushing pizza dough into a flat, round pan.

"Fine, thanks," said Ace. "You and Billy coming to the big game Friday night?"

"I bought some tickets to help raise

money for the playground," said Mr. Castello. "But Nonno and I have to keep the pizza parlor open. So Billy's going with his mom. She's a great sports fan. Ready to order?"

"I'll have two slices of the Basketball Special," said Ace.

The Basketball Special was pizza with everything on it. Salami, meatballs, sausage, cheese, mushrooms, peppers, and onions. Every season Mr. Castello changed the name of the Special. In the fall it was the Football Special. In the spring it was the Baseball Special. Now, in the winter, it was the Basketball Special.

"Two Basketballs coming up," said Billy's father.

Ace studied the baseball trophy on the cash register. The words on it said, "Spring Town Minor League Baseball Champs." Next to the big trophy was a smaller one. "Billy Castello," it said. "Most valuable player."

Ace smiled. "You really must have been

proud when Billy hit that grand slam," he said.

"That's my boy," said Billy's dad. "Someday Billy's going to get a baseball scholarship. What about you? You hoping for a basketball scholarship?"

Ace nodded. "Some college scouts are coming Friday night to see me play," he said. "I've got my fingers crossed."

"Where do you want to go?" asked Billy. "Seton Hall?"

"Duke," said Ace. "I've got the grades, but I don't know if I'm a good enough player for Duke. Still, that's my dream. I'm a Spring Town Tiger now. Maybe next year I'll be a Duke Blue Devil." Ace sighed. "To tell the truth, I'll go wherever I'm offered the most money. My parents can't afford college otherwise."

Nonno came over and leaned against the counter. He looked at Ace and said, "You never know what wonderful things are going to happen to you. When I am boy in Italy, my *mamma* get very sick. My sister very sick, too. My *papà* so worried. He afraid to leave them and go for medicine. I say, '*Papà*, don't worry. Let me go. Please, please, please!' He say, 'No, no, it's too far. You're too little.'"

Ace and the other basketball players ate their pizza and listened to Nonno's story. No other customers were in the pizza parlor. It was very quiet except for Nonno talking. "My father finally say okay," said Nonno.

"So off I go. I walk and walk. We live way out in the country. I walk down the road to town all by myself. I have such a good time! I stop to see the cows. I stop to watch the *farfalle*. How you say?"

"Butterflies," said Billy's dad.

"*Sì*, butterflies," said Nonno. "Finally I reach the doctor's house, and he give me bottle of medicine. I am so proud! I start to go home. I go down one street. I go down another. By now it is dark! I can't find the right street. I am lost.

"I stand in the street and cry. Cry and cry so loud. A man comes to the window and opens the shutters. He say to me, 'Little boy, what you doing here?'

"It is Bruno. One of the workers at my father's mill. I am so happy to see him. I cry some more.

"Bruno take me into his house. His wife

hug me. She give me a little something to eat. I put it into my mouth. And I stop crying."

Nonno looked at Ace and asked, "You know what she give me?"

"Not really," said Ace. Billy could tell he was a little embarrassed.

"Chocolate," said Nonno. "That was first

time in my life I ever eat chocolate. It was the most wonderful thing I ever eat! I still love it. Here."

Nonno reached under the counter. He grabbed a bunch of Italian chocolate bars and gave one to each person.

Billy felt his grandfather had lost track of the story. He decided to help him. "Then Bruno took you home?" he asked.

"Sure, sure," said Nonno. "And my mother and my sister get better. But that's not the point."

"What is the point?" asked Billy.

"Like I say," said Nonno. "You never know what wonderful things can happen to you. You get lost. You get scared. You cry. But never give up! Because life may have a surprise for you. Like chocolate. You see what I mean? You must always give life a chance!"

4 Practice, Practice, and More Practice

Wednesday morning Billy got up early and went outside to practice. It was freezing, but Billy didn't care. He stood about six feet away from the basket and threw the ball.

The basketball missed the pole completely. It hit the back of the pizza parlor with a thump. Billy stepped forward and threw again. The basketball missed and hit the building again.

Billy moved two steps to the right and

back a few inches. He threw the ball. It went into the peach basket. "All right!" he shouted.

A window shot up. Billy's father stuck his head out into the cold morning air. "What are you doing?" he asked.

"Practicing for Saturday!" said Billy.

"Before school? With a peach basket? Where did you get that, anyway?"

Billy just smiled.

"Why didn't you say you wanted a basket-ball hoop?" asked his father.

"I did," said Billy.

"When?"

"Last year."

Billy's father muttered *"Mamma mia"* and shut the window.

A few minutes later he came outside in his bathrobe. He watched Billy shoot.

"You're standing too stiff," he said. "Bend your legs a little."

Billy bent his legs and threw the ball. The ball hit the rim but didn't go in.

"Let *me* try," said his dad.

Billy chucked the ball to his father. His dad shot and missed, too.

"Bend your legs," said Billy.

His father laughed and tried again. He missed again. "I can't play in a bathrobe," he said. "It's too cold. Good luck to you. I'm going in."

Billy stood in his special place and bent his legs. He shot the ball at the peach basket. Again and again and again.

Every once in a while, he made a basket.

After school, Billy, Rosie, and Chris went to the pizza parlor to practice. Instead of a peach basket, they found a real basketball hoop on the light pole.

They ran into the pizza parlor. "Dad!" Billy said. "Thanks a lot!"

"You're welcome," said his dad.

"Did you ever play basketball, Mr. Castello?" asked Chris.

"Who, me?" said Billy's dad. "I'm too short. I stink at basketball."

"I stink, too," said Billy.

"No, Billy, you don't. You're getting better. You all are," said Mr. Castello.

Billy hoped his father was right.

On Thursday Billy, Chris, and Rosie practiced until it got dark. Billy's dad was right. They were getting better. But they wished they had more time. Slam Dunk Saturday was only two days away.

"We're not too bad behind the pizza parlor," said Rosie. "But how do we know how we'll do in the gym?"

"Yeah," said Billy. "We should practice somewhere else. Just to see what happens."

"Where?" asked Chris.

Billy's dad overheard them. He had come outside to watch.

Mr. Castello looked up at the navy-blue sky. The first stars of the evening were out. "After the dinner rush, I'll take you up to the playground," he said.

"The playground? At night? It's too dark—

and too cold," said Billy.

"There's no snow. And it won't be much colder than it is now," said his dad. "We'll only stay a little while. I'll turn the car lights on the court. Rosie and Chris, call your folks. Ask if you can have supper at the pizza parlor. Tell them I'll bring you home."

At seven-thirty Billy and his friends climbed into Mr. Castello's car. They rode to the school in silence. They couldn't believe a grownup was going to let them practice outside at night.

As they turned down the street by the playground, Billy saw a light.

"Someone's already there," he said.

For one horrid moment, Billy thought it was Chad.

But no, the person was taller. Billy opened the car door and heard organ music. The song was "Sweet Georgia Brown." It was the warm-up music for the Spring Town Tigers.

Four huge outdoor flashlights lit the playground. A portable tape player sat behind the hoop. Billy looked more carefully at the basketball player. It was Ace!

"Hi, Ace!" he called.

Ace stopped playing. "Who's there?" he called. "Hey! Hi, Billy. Hi, Mr. Castello. Hi, everyone. What are you doing here?"

"Same thing as you," said Billy. "Practicing."

"Great! Let's get to work," said Ace. He turned and shot the ball. It would have made a swish sound if there had been a net.

Ace worked at one end of the court. Billy and his friends worked at the other. No one spoke much. After a while, Ace came over and watched them.

Billy had been doing okay. But now that Ace was watching, he missed every shot.

"Don't be nervous," said Ace. "Just relax. Pretend you're all alone. Pretend no one is watching. Not even You Know Who."

Billy knew he meant Chad.

Billy imagined himself on a Chad-less court. All alone. He threw the ball. It went in.

"Perfect," said Ace. "Well, I'm taking off. Coming to the game tomorrow night?"

"Are you kidding?" said Billy.

"Yes," said Ace. "I'm kidding. I know you'll be there, Champ."

Champ! He said it again!

"Good luck, Ace," said Mr. Castello.

"Thanks," said Ace, shaking his hand. "You know why I came here tonight? I grew up playing ball on this playground. I figured being here tonight would calm me down."

"It sure calmed *me* down," thought Billy.

5 **The Big Game**

Friday night's game was being played in a real college gym. Rows and rows of bleachers rose like hills on all four sides. On one side the crowd held black-and-orange banners that said "Spring Town Tigers." On the other side people held blue-and-white banners that said "Elmwood Eagles".

Billy was with his mom. She loved basketball. His half sister Lily had stayed home with Billy's stepfather. She was too young for a high school basketball game. Billy was sorry not to see Lily and his stepfather. But he also liked being alone with his mom. They found seats halfway up the black-and-orange side.

"Let's save seats for Rosie and Chris," said Billy. He watched the door. Soon he saw them. Billy waved, and they waved back. They came up with their parents and sat down.

"Ladies and gentlemen!" said the announcer. "The Elmwood Eagles!"

From one corner of the floor came a line of blue. It was the Elmwood team in electric-blue warm-up suits. Big white eagles were printed on the back of their jackets. Everyone on the other side of the gym stood up and roared. The Elmwood cheerleaders waved blue-and-white pom-poms.

The Elmwood players shot baskets at one of the hoops.

"Ladies and gentlemen!" said the announcer. "The Spring Town Tigers!"

From the other corner of the floor came the sound of "Sweet Georgia Brown." The Spring Town team ran in. They were dressed in orange warm-up suits. Everyone on Billy's side of the gym stood up and roared like tigers. Billy and his mom joined in. The crowd was so large, they couldn't hear their own voices. The Spring Town cheerleaders waved black-and-orange pom-poms.

The Spring Town players warmed up to the music. Ace made every basket. "Way to go, Ace!" shouted Billy.

After a while the players went and sat on the bench. Then the game started. A Spring Town player dribbled up the floor and passed to Ace. Ace made a basket. The Spring Town fans roared again. The score was 2–0, Spring Town.

Elmwood got the ball. They took it up the court and also scored. Now the score was 2–2. And that's the way the game went. Spring Town players would score. And Spring Town fans would cheer.

But then Elmwood players would score. And Elmwood fans would cheer. At the end of the first quarter the score was tied 14–14.

"I'm getting nervous," said Billy's mom.

Billy was a little worried, too. Ace had been great on defense, but he had made only six points.

But in the second quarter Ace scored ten points all by himself.

"That kid's amazing," said Billy's mom.

"I know him," said Billy.

"We all know him," shouted someone behind him.

Billy turned and saw Chad. Where had he come from? He hadn't been sitting there before.

Chad was with his older brother and some other high school kids. They were very loud. They booed at everything the Elmwood players did.

Billy and his mom tried to ignore them. But it was hard. It was like trying to ignore a bunch of gorillas.

Finally, Billy's mother turned around and said, "Would you mind not yelling right in my ear?"

A few minutes later Chad and the high school boys moved to the top row. Billy could still hear them. He was so embarrassed! He could just imagine what would happen on Monday. If Billy yelled on the playground, Chad would say, "Would you mind not yelling right in my ear?"

The buzzer sounded. It was halftime. The score was 35–30 in favor of Spring Town. The Spring Town fans stood up and roared like crazy.

During halftime Spring Town parents sold food and school caps in the hall. Billy and his mom each got a soda. Then she bought him a Spring Town Tiger cap. "How's school going?" she asked.

"Good," said Billy. "How's Lily?"

"Fine," said his mom. "She had a cold last week."

"That's too bad," said Billy.

"How's your dad?"

"Fine," said Billy.

Then they were silent. It was always hard

to talk with his mother about his father. His parents had been divorced for four years. Billy was sort of used to it. But he felt funny when they asked about each other.

"Want to go back in?" asked his mom.

"Okay," said Billy.

Spring Town stayed ahead of Elmwood for most of the third quarter. Ace was hot. He scored ten more points. Billy was so proud of him!

But in the fourth quarter something went wrong. Spring Town slipped behind by two points. The score was 56–54 in favor of Elmwood.

Then Elmwood scored, and Spring Town was behind by four points, 58–54! Then Elmwood scored again, and Spring Town fell behind by six points.

The Spring Town coach called a time-out. The Spring Town cheerleaders ran onto the floor and shouted, "Gimme a T!"

"T!" yelled the fans. But not Billy. He was watching Ace.

Ace was sitting on a chair. His head was down between his knees. He was breathing hard. Someone handed him a towel. Ace wiped his face and listened to the coach.

The coach was yelling at him. He was yelling at all the players. The players looked really scared.

Billy felt scared, too.

"You think we'll win?" he asked his mom.

"I don't know," she said. She was biting her lip.

"Of course, we'll win," said Rosie.

"There are only two minutes left!" said Billy.

"Two minutes is a lot of time in basketball," said his mom.

The game began again.

Spring Town had the ball. Ace faked to one side and then passed to another player. This player ran and made a great lay-up. The crowd roared. Spring Town was now down by only four!

Elmwood had the ball. They raced up the court. Their best player aimed and fired. Someone jumped up and blocked the ball. It was Ace!

The Spring Town fans cheered again. "Go, Tigers! Go, Tigers!"

Now Spring Town had the ball. They passed. They dribbled. Ace made an amazing jump shot from the base line. In! The score was 60–58!

"All right, Ace!" shouted Billy. "Two points to go!"

There were only 16 seconds left. Elmwood had the ball. Their players passed it safely back and forth. They weren't taking any chances.

"Get that ball! Get that ball!" yelled the Spring Town fans.

Ace leaped between two players and grabbed the ball.

"Yes!" yelled Billy.

Immediately, an Elmwood player bumped

into Ace. Ace fell down. The whistle blew. "Foul! One and one!" yelled the referee.

Ace walked to the foul line. The pressure was on him now. If he made his first shot, he would get to shoot the second. Spring Town was two points behind. He had to make both shots to tie the game.

"Ace won't miss," said Billy.

"I hope not," said his mom.

Ace dribbled the ball. The Elmwood fans were booing him like crazy. The Spring Town fans were completely silent. Even Chad.

The clock showed only one second to go. But right now it didn't matter. The clock didn't run when players took foul shots.

Ace wiped his forehead. He dribbled the ball some more. Then he stopped. He took a deep breath. And another deep breath. Then he lifted the ball up into the air and gave it a push.

The ball sailed toward the basket and landed on the rim. It twirled round and round and round....

"Please go in!" prayed Billy.

The ball fell in. The score was now 60–59. Billy, his mom, Chris, Rosie, and all the other Tiger fans roared. And then they fell silent again.

The Elmwood fans were booing louder than ever.

"Don't listen to them," thought Billy. "Remember what you told me. Pretend they're not there. You're all alone." Billy crossed his fingers. He showed them to Chris and Rosie. They crossed their fingers, too. So did his mother.

"I know he's going to make it," said Billy. "Then we'll win in overtime."

Ace dribbled the ball.

Some fans on the Elmwood side started to sing.

> *"Nah, nah,*
> *Nah, nah, nah, nah,*
> *Hey, hey, hey,*
> *Go home."*

Ace stopped dribbling. He took a deep breath. Dribbled again. Took another deep breath. Dribbled again. Then he lifted the ball up into the air. And tossed it.

The ball took forever to sail through the air. Then it hit the rim and bounced off.

An Elmwood player caught the rebound. The final buzzer sounded.

"We did it!" shouted the Elmwood player. "We won!"

It was true.

Elmwood had won, 60–59.

Other Elmwood Eagles jumped on top of the player with the ball. They all fell to the floor in a big blue-and-white pile. "We did it! We won!" they hollered.

Ace dropped to the floor, too. Right on the foul line. All by himself. His shoulders were shaking. Other Spring Town players fell to the floor, too.

"Are they hurt?" asked Billy.

"No," said his mom. "Just broken-hearted.

Poor guys. They tried so hard, and they wanted to win so much."

His mother squeezed his hand. Billy opened his eyes as wide as he could to keep them dry.

6 Slam Dunk Saturday

The next morning the alarm clock on the stove woke Billy up. His new orange Tiger cap was sitting on the kitchen counter. Billy stared at it and felt sick.

It was nine o'clock. Slam Dunk Saturday started at ten.

Billy shut his eyes. He could still see Ace crying on the basketball court. He hadn't cried for long. After a minute, he had stood up and gone over to the coach. The coach gave him a hug. He had given all the Tigers hugs.

There was a brief ceremony after the game. The Elmwood players got big trophies. The Spring Town players got small trophies. The blue players and the orange players shook hands.

But that was last night. Now Billy had to get up. He had to go to the school gym. He had to be in the Shoot-Out Contest.

What a nightmare! No matter how much he had practiced, he'd never be able to make a basket now.

He felt too rotten.

Everyone there would feel rotten.

Especially Ace.

Poor Ace. He had lost the big game. Billy knew just how he would feel. He would feel that he had let his school down. That he had let the whole town down. That he would never get a college scholarship now.

Ace would probably stay home this morning.

That's what Billy felt like doing.

But he couldn't. Billy dragged himself out of bed and took a shower. Then he went downstairs to the pizza parlor. His father and Nonno were quiet.

Nonno made Billy some toast and scrambled eggs. He put an Italian chocolate bar on the plate, too.

"What's that for?" asked Billy.

"For Ace," said Nonno. "Tell him to remember the chocolate story. Even when you're down, give life a chance!"

Billy stuck the chocolate bar in his pocket. But he didn't know why. What was the point of taking it to Ace if Ace wasn't going to be there?

The mood in the Spring Town gym was quiet. People chatted sadly about the big game.

Rosie's mother had made a sign with a thermometer on it. The thermometer measured how much money had been raised for the playground. Right now the line was colored up to the $2,000 mark. "Cheer up!" she said. "We have made two thousand dollars so far! We have just one thousand to go. If we reach three thousand, we can start building the new playground in May!"

Billy found Chris and Rosie. They sat down on the floor in front of another sign. It listed the rules for the Shoot-Out Contest.

They didn't feel like reading them.

Chad entered the gym and walked over. "Did you hear?" he said. "I have more pledges than anyone in our age group. I'll make ten dollars a basket! I bet I make more money than all of you! Any of you squirts brave enough to bet against me?"

Nobody said a word.

"You're all chickens," said Chad. *"Peep, peep, peep!"*

The kids pretended they didn't hear him. They watched Rosie's mother. She and some of the other grownups were walking to the microphone.

Finally, Rosie's mother spoke into the

mike. "As you know," she said, "the Spring Town Tigers lost by one point last night. It was a heart-wrenching game. The players were supposed to run the contests today, but they haven't come yet. They probably feel too sad to come. We understand."

Everyone clapped for the Tigers even though they weren't there to hear.

"We've decided to start the Shoot-Out Contest without them," said Rosie's mother. "Okay? So let's cheer up and get going. If you're in the first division, go to the far basket. Second division, please come to the basket near me."

Billy, Chris, Rosie, Chad, and some other kids stood under their basket. Rosie's mother wrote down their names and pledges on a blackboard.

Chris wanted to get it over with so he went first. He had five dollars in pledges for each basket. In one minute he made four baskets.

"Four times five," said Rosie's mother.

"That's twenty dollars! Hooray for Chris!"

"Hey!" said a voice. "That's my job."

Everyone turned. It was Ace! And all the other Spring Town Tigers! They were dressed in old black sweat pants and orange warm-up jerseys.

Ace took the chalk from Rosie's mother and gave her a hug. She gave him a big hug back.

Ace went up to the microphone. He started to speak and stopped. Then he started

again. "Listen up, everyone," he said. He took a deep breath and went on. "I speak for all the guys on the team. Thanks for your support."

Ace and the high school players started to clap. Everyone in the gym started to clap, too. No one knew exactly what they were clapping for. Basketball? Sports? Spring Town? Friendship? The noise was sad, but people felt better.

"Okay!" said Ace. "Let's make some money

here today! We need a new playground!"

"Yeah!" shouted the basketball players.

"I have six dollars pledged for each basket I make in the Shoot-Out," said Ace. "Anyone who wants to pledge more, sign up now!"

A few minutes later Ace had $20 pledged for each basket. Even Billy pledged. For every basket that Ace made, Billy promised to pay him ten cents.

"Great!" said Ace. "And now let's go on with the contest!"

Rosie was very brave. She volunteered to go next. She had four dollars' worth of pledges and made eight baskets.

"Eight times four is thirty-two dollars for Rosie!" said Ace. He wrote the amount next to her name on the blackboard.

After a few more players, it was Chad's turn. Chad told Ace he would earn ten dollars a basket.

"Terrific," said Ace. "Go to it!"

Chad took the ball and stood at half

court. He dribbled with his right hand down the court. Then he switched to his left hand. He dribbled this way and that. He looked to see if Ace was watching. He was. Chad stopped and jumped. He made the basket.

Chad caught the rebound. He dribbled to the right and to the left. He was pretending he was in a game. He spun around with the ball and threw a beautiful hook shot. Unfortunately, it missed.

Chad ran up and caught the rebound. He dribbled down the base line. He even dribbled behind his back! No doubt about it. Chad could dribble better than anyone else in elementary school.

He made a fancy lay-up. It went in.

"Wow," said Billy. "He's good."

"Yeah," said Chris. "But he's wasting time. The whole point is to make money. The more baskets you make, the more money for the playground."

It was true. Chad was impressing everyone with his ball handling. But he wasn't making as many baskets as he could. When his minute was up, he had only made 12 baskets.

"Twelve times ten," said Ace. "One hundred and twenty dollars for Chad!"

That was a lot of money. Chad looked really proud of himself.

It was Billy's turn now. His dad had kicked in two more dollars per basket. So Billy now had five dollars in pledges per basket. Ace tossed him the ball and winked.

Billy walked over to the basket. He held the ball up.

"Go!" said Ace.

Billy shot. He missed. "You stink!" he told himself. The ball bounced back to him. He shot again and missed again. "You idiot!"

He could hear Chad snickering. This was worse than Billy had imagined.

Billy dribbled the ball and tried to concentrate. "What's the matter with you?" he

asked himself. He realized he was still thinking about Ace. He was still thinking of how
Ace had missed that last basket.

But Ace had gotten over it. Billy had to
get over it, too.

Billy thought of how much Ace had
helped him. He didn't want to let Ace down
now. He tried to remember Ace's advice. Find
your spot. Take a breath. Shoot. Billy
stopped dribbling and shot again. This time
he made a basket.

Get a rhythm, Ace had said. Billy caught
the ball and shot. He made another basket!
He kept going. He was like a machine now.
Over and over he caught the ball and shot.
He missed a few, but he didn't let his mis-
takes get to him.

By the time his minute was up, he had
made 25 baskets!

"Twenty-five times five is one hundred
and twenty-five dollars!" said Ace.

Ace looked over the results on the black-

board. Then he announced, "And the winners in the second division are: Billy Castello for the most money earned and Billy Castello for the most baskets made!"

Billy couldn't believe it. He had made more baskets than Chad! He had beat the best and tallest basketball player in elementary school.

Ace came over and slapped him a high five. "You're a champ, kid," he said. "A real champ."

All the players in Billy's age group gave him high fives, too. Everyone except Chad. "You cheated," said Chad. "You just stood in the same place and shot. That's how wimps do it."

"No," said Ace. "That's how people who want to raise a lot of money for the playground do it."

"Oh, yeah?" said Chad. "How are *you* going to do it?"

"I'm doing it Billy's way," said Ace.

And that's just what Ace did. When it was Ace's turn, he stood in Billy's spot. He made 50 baskets! Everyone cheered like crazy.

"Fifty times twenty is...one thousand dollars! Thank you, Ace!" screamed Rosie's mother into the microphone. "Spring Town has now raised over three thousand dollars!"

Rosie colored the thermometer up to the top and beyond.

As people were clapping, a stranger entered the gym. He had on a blue jacket. It said "Duke" on the back.

"Ace!" said Billy. "Look! There's someone here from Duke!"

Ace looked over. His face turned white. The man was looking around the gym. When he saw Ace, he waved. He came over to Ace and shook his hand.

"I tried to call you last night," he said. "I'm from Duke University. Is your phone broken?"

"I took it off the hook," said Ace.

"Well, put it back on. The Duke basketball coach may give you a call next week. You played a mighty fine game last night. Don't worry about that last shot. Nobody's perfect."

Ace shook the man's hand again and grinned from ear to ear.

7 After the Contests

When the basketball contests were over, everybody swarmed around Ace. They congratulated him for raising so much money and for the news about Duke.

Billy put on his jacket and waited at the edge of the crowd. He noticed Chad standing nearby. Billy didn't mind. Chad didn't bother him anymore.

At last, when most people had gone, Billy reached up and gave Ace a hug.

Ace hugged Billy back and lifted him up into the air. "You know who I feel like?" he asked.

"Who?" asked Billy.

Ace set him down. "Remember your grandpa's Italian chocolate story? Last night I felt like the little boy who got lost. Now I feel like the boy who was found."

"After he tasted his first piece of chocolate," said Billy.

"You got it, Champ," said Ace.

"What are you guys talking about?" asked Chad. He was standing behind Ace and Billy.

Ace and Billy turned around.

"We're talking about Italian chocolate," said Ace. "It's the best. If I had some, I'd give it to you. You were great today."

"Are you kidding?" said Chad. "I blew it. I lost."

"Well, you were great even though you lost," said Ace. "You know what, Chad? All you need is time. Time to learn more about basketball. And time to learn about being a good sport. Then you're going to be one heck of a basketball player."

"Better than me," said Billy.

Chad looked down at Billy with surprise. "I guess I should congratulate you," he said. Chad held out his hand.

Billy shook it. Then he put his hands in his pocket. "Hey!" he said. "Look what I found!" Billy pulled out the Italian chocolate bar. "Nonno sent this for you, Ace."

"And I'm going to give it to Chad," said Ace. "In honor of all the wonderful things that can happen to you. As long as you give life a chance."

Chad looked puzzled. But he took the candy bar.

Ace waved to his parents and friends across the gym. "I have to go," he said. "See you around, guys."

Billy and Chad were alone in the middle of the gym. They looked at each other.

"You want some of this chocolate?" asked Chad.

"Tell you what," said Billy. "Let's go get some pizza first."

About the Author

"I've never played basketball on a real school team. But I loved shooting baskets in my driveway as a kid. Now I enjoy watching basketball games," says JEAN MARZOLLO. "Basketball is *always* fast-paced—whether the players are kids in my town or the New York Knicks!" Jean Marzollo is the author of dozens of books for children, including *Red Ribbon Rosie, The Pizza Pie Slugger,* and the popular I Spy books. She lives in Cold Spring, New York, with her husband and two sons.

About the Illustrator

"I was always one of the shortest kids in my class," says BLANCHE SIMS. "To everybody's surprise, I became a really good basketball player—just like Billy!" Blanche Sims has illustrated more than 75 children's books, including *Red Ribbon Rosie* and *The Pizza Pie Slugger,* both Stepping Stone Books by Jean Marzollo. She lives in Westport, Connecticut.